MINI CLASSICS
THE
STEADFAST
TIN SOLDIER

RETOLD BY STEPHANIE LASLETT
ILLUSTRATED BY HELEN SMITH

PARRAGON

TITLES IN SERIES I AND III OF THE
MINI CLASSICS INCLUDE:

SERIES III

A PARRAGON BOOK

Published by
Parragon Books,
Unit 13–17, Avonbridge Trading Estate,
Atlantic Road, Avonmouth, Bristol BS11 9QD

Produced by
The Templar Company plc,
Pippbrook Mill, London Road, Dorking, Surrey RH4 1JE

Copyright © 1994 Parragon Books Service Limited

Designed by Mark Kingsley-Monks

Printed and bound in Great Britain

ISBN 1-85813-719-5

There were once upon a time five-and-twenty tin soldiers — all brothers, for they were made out of the same old tin spoon. Dressed in a smart red uniform, each one carried a gun upon

his shoulder and looked
straight ahead with a
brave and steady gaze.
They lay side by side in
a wooden box and the
first words that they
heard when the lid was
lifted off, were,
"Hurray, tin soldiers!"

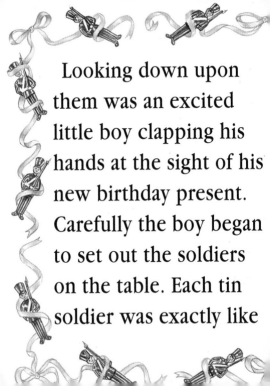

Looking down upon them was an excited little boy clapping his hands at the sight of his new birthday present. Carefully the boy began to set out the soldiers on the table. Each tin soldier was exactly like

the other in every way,
except just one. He had
been made last of all
when the tin ran out
and so he had only one
leg, but there he stood
as firm and steadfast on
his one leg as the others
did on two.

This is the Tin Soldier
who became famous, as
you will soon see.

As the soldiers stood straight and tall, glad to be freed from their box at last, they could see something else upon the table. Close by was a pretty little castle made of cardboard. It had proper windows so

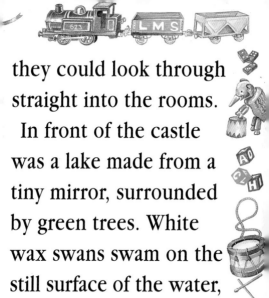

they could look through
straight into the rooms.

In front of the castle
was a lake made from a
tiny mirror, surrounded
by green trees. White
wax swans swam on the
still surface of the water,
admiring their reflections.

Now this was all very pretty, but the most beautiful thing of all was a sweet little lady who stood in the open doorway of the castle. She was made of paper, but wore a soft white dress of the finest muslin.

A scarf of narrow blue
ribbon was draped
round her shoulders
and pinned together at
the front of her bodice
with a glittering rose
brooch made of gold
paper. It was almost as
large as her head!

The little lady stood beautifully tall and straight and carried her arms high above her head, for she was a Dancer.

The Dancer held one graceful leg so high in the air that the Tin Soldier couldn't see it at all and so he decided that she had only one leg, just like him.

"That's the wife for me!" he thought. Then

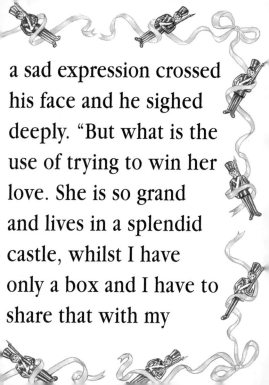

a sad expression crossed his face and he sighed deeply. "But what is the use of trying to win her love. She is so grand and lives in a splendid castle, whilst I have only a box and I have to share that with my twenty four brothers. This is no place for her!" and the poor Tin Soldier sighed again as he gazed at the lovely lady. "But she is so very beautiful! I must at least meet her and say hello." All that day the Soldier

stood tall and straight behind a snuff box that lay on the table and from there he had a clear view of the dainty little Dancer, who continued to stand on one leg without ever losing her balance.

When the day was over, the little boy carefully packed his Tin Soldiers away in their box and didn't notice that one of them was missing. As night fell, the dark house grew still and soon everyone was fast asleep.

Then it was time for
the toys to play! Up they
jumped and danced and
fought, and merrily
laughed and sang.

The Tin Soldiers could hear all the noise and they rattled and jostled against one another for they longed to join in the fun. But no matter how much they shook their box they could not raise the lid and so

had to lie there alone
in the dark, listening to
the other toys having a
wonderful time while
their shadows danced
on the walls.

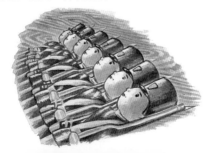

The nutcrackers
played at leap-frog and
the slate pencil ran all
over the slate! There
was such a noise that
the canary woke up and
began to chatter and
sing to them all, and in
poetry too!

The only two toys who did not stir from their places were the Tin Soldier and the little Dancer. She remained on tip-toe, with both arms outstretched; he stood steadfastly on his one leg and his eyes

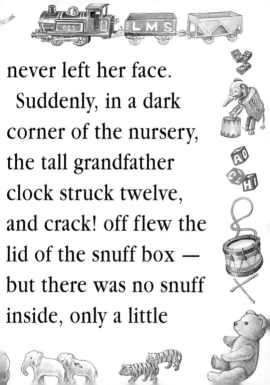

never left her face.
Suddenly, in a dark
corner of the nursery,
the tall grandfather
clock struck twelve,
and crack! off flew the
lid of the snuff box —
but there was no snuff
inside, only a little

black imp who popped
up just like a jack-in-
the-box.

"Hello, Tin Soldier!"
said the imp. "Why are
you looking at the little
Dancer? Don't you
know that it's rather
rude to stare?"

33

But the Tin Soldier took no notice. He acted as if he had heard nothing at all.

"Very well then," cried the imp, stamping his foot, "but you just wait till tomorrow!" and with that, he jumped

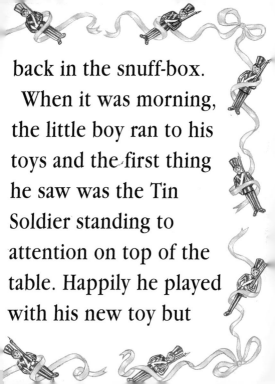

back in the snuff-box.
When it was morning,
the little boy ran to his
toys and the first thing
he saw was the Tin
Soldier standing to
attention on top of the
table. Happily he played
with his new toy but

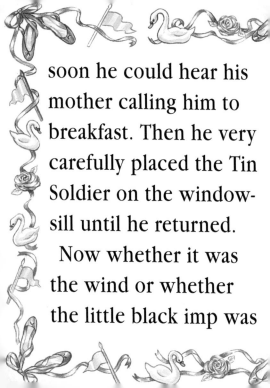

soon he could hear his
mother calling him to
breakfast. Then he very
carefully placed the Tin
Soldier on the window-
sill until he returned.

Now whether it was
the wind or whether
the little black imp was

up to his tricks, I do not know, but all at once the window flew open with a bang, the curtains flapped and out fell the little Tin Soldier, tumbling head over heels, from the third storey nursery window!

That was a terrible fall
for the little Tin Soldier,
I can tell you! With a
bump he landed upside
down with his leg in
the air and there he
stayed, for his gun was
firmly wedged between
two paving-stones.

When the little boy returned and saw the window wide open and his favourite toy missing he guessed what had happened and quickly ran outside with the nursery-maid to search for the poor Tin Soldier.

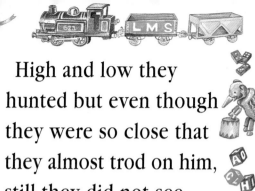

High and low they hunted but even though they were so close that they almost trod on him, still they did not see him stuck upside down between the paving stones.

If the Tin Soldier had

only called out "Here I am!" they would have easily found him, but he could not bring himself to shout because he was wearing his smart uniform and he thought a soldier should be able to take care of himself.

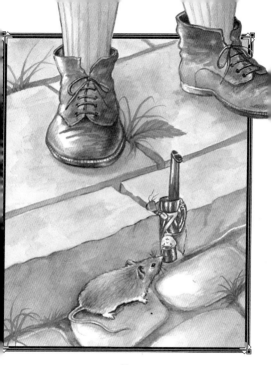

43

Soon the sky grew grey and it began to drizzle. The raindrops fell faster and before long there was a regular steady downpour.

When the rain stopped, two little street urchins came along and soon they spotted the poor Tin Soldier.

"Just look!" cried one. "Here is a Tin Soldier! Let's make him a boat and then he shall sail up

and down like a fine Sea
Admiral of the Fleet!"
 So they made a little
boat out of newspaper
and the Tin Soldier
sailed up and down the
gutter whilst the boys
ran along beside him,
clapping their hands.

But what great waves
there were in the
gutter! The paper boat
was tossed up and
down and carried along
so swiftly that the Tin
Soldier trembled, but
he remained steadfast
and showed no fear.

All of a sudden the boat entered a long tunnel! The boys' excited cries faded away behind him with the light and soon it was just as dark as his box had been. "Where am I going now?"

wondered the little Tin Soldier. "Oh, dear! This is all the fault of that black imp! If only the little Dancer were sitting beside me here in the boat, it could be twice as dark for all I should care!"

Suddenly a great water rat poked his head out of the water alongside the paper boat and glared at the Tin Soldier.

"Have you a passport?" he demanded. "Come on — let me see your papers immediately!"

But the Tin Soldier never flinched. Silently he stared ahead and grasped his gun even more firmly than before.

The boat sped on down the dark tunnel with the huge rat swimming close behind.

Ugh! He was fierce and ugly and bared his sharp teeth as he called out to the scraps of rubbish floating along beside the boat. "Stop the Tin Soldier! Stop him! He has not paid the toll or shown his passport!"

The current in the water became swifter and stronger. Ahead of him the Tin Soldier was greatly relieved to see a glimpse of daylight at the end of the tunnel — but what was that terrible roaring noise?

He could hear the rushing of water, quite enough to frighten any brave man. Ahead of him the gutter emptied out into a great canal and for the poor Tin Soldier, that rush and tumble of water was

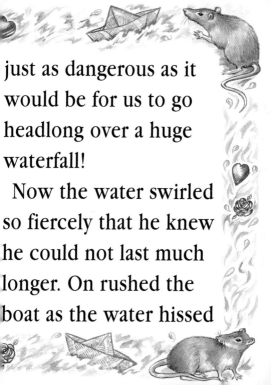

just as dangerous as it would be for us to go headlong over a huge waterfall!

Now the water swirled so fiercely that he knew he could not last much longer. On rushed the boat as the water hissed

and boiled around him
and the noise grew ever
louder in his ears.

Suddenly the paper
boat whirled four times
around, and as the water
rushed in over its sides,
it began to sink! Then
the poor little Tin

Soldier stood straight to attention as best he could, for he wanted to be sure that no-one would ever be able to say afterwards that he had been a coward. There he stood, up to his neck in water, as the paper grew soggier and the boat sank deeper.

At last the cold water crept right over the top of his head and all he could think of was the pretty little Dancer whose face he should never see again.

As he sank into the
murky depths he heard
a voice inside his head.
"Forward, forward,
soldier bold!
Death's before thee,
grim and cold!"
With that, the paper
boat fell apart and the

soldier fell down, down
— and at that moment
was swallowed up by a
great fish!

Oh! how dark it was
inside the fish, even
darker than it had been
in the tunnel, and it was
such a tight squash!

But there the steadfast little Tin Soldier lay full length, still shouldering his gun.

70

Up and down swam
the fish, then all at once
he began to twist and
thrash in the water. But
just as soon as he had
begun, the fish stopped
moving and became
quite still. The Soldier
lay quietly for a long

time, not knowing where he was or what would become of him.

Then like a flash of lightning, bright daylight streamed over him, and a voice exclaimed, "Why, here is a little Tin Soldier!"

The Soldier had had quite a journey. The fish had been caught on a fisherman's hook, taken to market, sold, and was now lying silver-bright on a kitchen table ready to be cooked. What a surprise the

cook had when she saw
the Tin Soldier lying
ramrod straight in
the fish's belly, still
shouldering his gun!
  She picked him up
between her finger and
thumb, and carried him
into the nursery, where

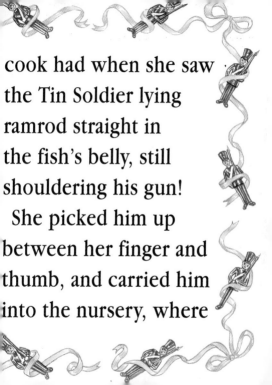

everyone wanted to see
the hero who had been
found inside a fish —
but the Tin Soldier did
not feel at all proud.

They put him on the
table, and — well, but
what strange things do
happen in this world!

The Tin Soldier was in
the very same room in
which he had once
shared a box with his
twenty four brothers!
He saw the same little
boy and there was the
same grand castle with
the pretty little Dancer.

She was still standing on one leg with the other high in the air, for she too was steadfast.

That moved the Tin
Soldier and he felt as if
he might shed tin-tears,
but that would not have
been fitting for a soldier.
He looked over at her,
and she looked straight
back at him, but she
said nothing.

All at once the little boy picked up the Tin Soldier and threw him into the fire!

Why did he do it?
Nobody knew, but
doubtless the little black
imp in the snuff box
had something to do
with this new bit of
mischief, too.

There stood the Tin
Soldier, unflinching.

He balanced on his one leg right in the middle of the fire and the heat was truly terrible, but whether it was the pain of the flames or the pain of the love in his heart, he did not know for sure.

All his colour had
worn off, and whether
this had happened on
his long journey or
whether it was the
result of his sorrow,
who can say?

He looked straight at
the little lady and she

looked straight at him,
and he felt that he was
melting, but still he
remained steadfast,
with his gun at his
shoulder. Suddenly the
door opened and a cold
draught blew the little
Dancer off the table.

She flew into the air and floated just like thistledown straight to the Tin Soldier standing steadfast in the fire and as her arms brushed his cheeks, she instantly burst into flames. Then the Tin Soldier finally

93

softened and began to
melt in the hot flames.

Next morning when
the maid came to clear
away the ashes, she
found a small lump of
tin in the shape of a
heart — all that was left
of the little Tin Soldier.

And all that was left of
the little Dancer was her
golden rose, burnt as
black as a cinder of coal.

Hans Christian Anderson

Hans Andersen was born in Odense,
Denmark on April 2nd, 1805. His family
was very poor and throughout his life he
suffered much unhappiness. Even after he had
found success as a writer, Hans Andersen
felt something of an outsider; an
attitude which often emerged in his stories,
such as here in *The Steadfast Tin Soldier*,
published in 1838.
His fairy stories, famous throughout the
world, include *The Snow Queen*, *The Little
Mermaid* and *The Emperor's New Clothes*,
and are amongst the most frequently
translated works of literature.
He died in 1875.